WARRIORS

TIGERSTAR & SASHA

#2: ESCAPE FROM
THE FOREST

WARRIORS
TIGERSTAR & SASHA
#2: ESCAPE FROM THE FOREST

CREATED BY
ERIN HUNTER

WRITTEN BY
DAN JOLLEY

ART BY
DON HUDSON

TOKYOPOP®

HAMBURG // LONDON // LOS ANGELES // TOKYO

HarperCollinsPublishers

Warriors: Tigerstar and Sasha Vol. 2:
Escape from the Forest
Created by Erin Hunter
Written by Dan Jolley
Art by Don Hudson

Cover Colorist - Jason Van Winkle
Digital Tones - Lincy Chan
Lettering - Michael Paolilli
Cover Design - Tina Corrales

Editor - Jenna Winterberg
Pre-Production Supervisor - Vicente Rivera, Jr.
Print-Production Specialist - Lucas Rivera
Managing Editor - Vy Nguyen
Senior Designer - Louis Csontos
Senior Designer - James Lee
Senior Editor - Bryce P. Coleman
Senior Editor - Jenna Winterberg
Associate Publisher - Marco F. Pavia
President and C.O.O. - John Parker
C.E.O. and Chief Creative Officer - Stuart Levy

A **TOKYOPOP** Manga

TOKYOPOP and ⟨logo⟩ are trademarks or registered trademarks of TOKYOPOP Inc.

TOKYOPOP Inc.
5900 Wilshire Blvd. Suite 2000
Los Angeles, CA 90036

E-mail: info@TOKYOPOP.com
Come visit us online at www.TOKYOPOP.com

For information address HarperCollins Children's Books, a division of HarperCollins Publishers,
10 East 53rd Street, New York, NY 10022
www.harpercollinschildrens.com

ISBN 978-0-06-154793-5
Library of Congress catalog card number: 2008904113

13 LP/BVG 10 9 8 7
❖
First Edition

Dear readers,

Tigerstar didn't only betray the four Clans; he also betrayed the cat who loved him most—brave, hopeful, innocent Sasha. She fell for a warrior with the courage of a lion, only to discover that he was fox-hearted and treacherous to the tip of his tail. Luckily for Sasha, she left the forest before the battle with BloodClan, so she didn't see the full extent of Tigerstar's brutal ambitions, or his dramatic death (nine times over) beneath Scourge's strengthened claws. Right now, her priority is finding a new way of life, far from the forest where she had made her home. Once again, she has lost everything but her will to survive.

This time, help comes from a very unexpected quarter. One thing I admire most about Sasha is her strength of spirit. She's always ready to see kindness and warmth in other characters—which might have been her downfall where Tigerstar was concerned! Don't judge her harshly: Too often, characters that suffer the most become very cynical and resistant to signs of affection. Even when Sasha realizes that her life has become even more complicated, she never gives up hope.

Come, it's time to find out what happened when Sasha stumbled away fom ShadowClan with her heart broken into pieces. . . .

Best wishes always,
Erin Hunter

I THOUGHT YOU UNDERSTOOD HOW IMPORTANT BEING LEADER OF MY CLAN IS TO ME.

I DO. BUT WHAT YOU'RE TRYING TO DO GOES FAR BEYOND THAT--

BEYOND THE WARRIOR CODE YOU'VE TOLD ME ABOUT, TOO.

HOW CAN YOU CONSIDER KILLING ALL THE CATS THAT WEREN'T BORN IN THE FOREST?

OR WHOSE PARENTS COME FROM DIFFERENT CLANS?

THAT'S NOT THEIR FAULT!

PLUS, UH, IF YOU'RE WORRIED...Y'KNOW, ABOUT BUMPING INTO ANY CLAN CATS...THERE'RE PLACES I CAN SHOW YOU.

DEEPER IN THE WOODS, I MEAN. THAT'S THE THING ABOUT THEIR BORDERS. THE CLANS DON'T CROSS THEM MUCH.

THANK YOU, PINE. IT'S VERY SWEET OF YOU TO OFFER.

BUT I HAVE TO FIND MY HOUSEFOLK. HIS NAME IS KEN, AND...

AND HE MUST BE MISSING ME TERRIBLY.

ALL RIGHT. WELL...

GOOD LUCK, SASHA. I REALLY HOPE YOU CAN FIND HIM.

I HOPE SO, TOO.

RIGHT NOW, KEN IS THE ONLY PART OF MY LIFE THAT MEANS ANYTHING.

THE SMELL OF PREY STARTLES ME SO MUCH, AT FIRST I THINK I'M DREAMING AGAIN.

IT'S COMING FROM THAT PLACE.

OH...I'VE GOT TO BE DREAMING...

THERE'S SO MUCH FOOD IN HERE! IT'S LIKE A GIANT FRESH-KILL PILE! I HAD NO IDEA HOUSEFOLK ATE THIS SORT OF THING!

SURELY THEY WON'T MIND IF I TAKE A BIT...

...JUST A LITTLE TINY BIT...

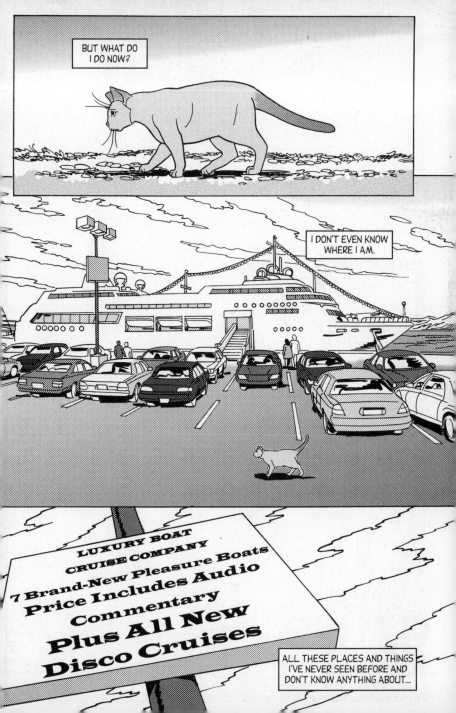

≈SNIFF≈
≈SNIFF≈

OH! THAT'S SOMETHING I KNOW ABOUT.

THAT'S HOUSEFOLK FOOD! AND MY STOMACH HURTS, IT'S SO EMPTY.

MAYBE IF I SNEAK IN...DON'T LET ANYBODY SEE ME... MAYBE I CAN FIND SOME SCRAP OF SOMETHING...

WHOOOO-HOOOO!!!

DID YOU SEE THAT, THE WAY SHANNON HURLED?

AWESOME, MAN, PURE AWESOME!

WHAT KIND OF PLACE IS THIS? ALL THOSE HOUSEFOLK WERE SO LOUD!

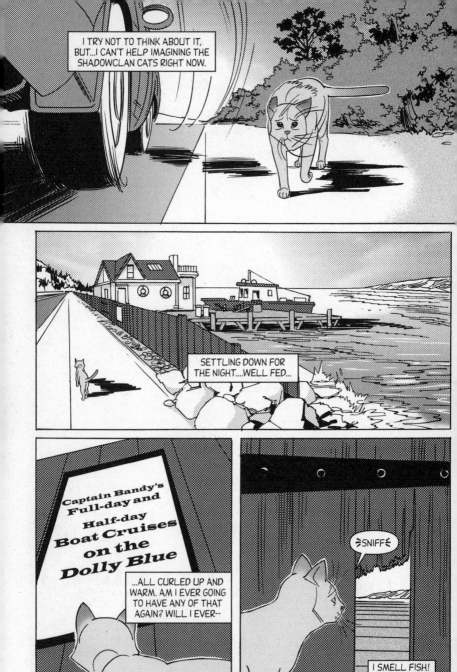

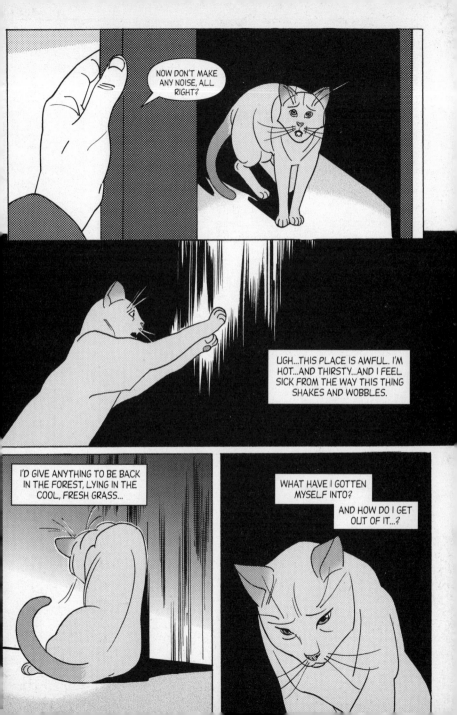

MUCH AS I HATED BEING LOCKED UP... WHEN I LOOK AT THE HOUSEFOLK'S OLD, WRINKLED FACE...

...I CAN'T HELP THINKING THAT HE REMINDS ME OF KEN. I CAN TELL HE'S LONELY AND SAD.

MAYBE NOT THE KIND OF SAD KEN WAS AFTER JEAN WENT AWAY...BUT STILL SAD.

I FEEL SORT OF SORRY FOR HIM.

THAT DOESN'T MAKE ME FEEL ANY BETTER, THOUGH. I REALLY WISH THE GROUND WOULD QUIT SWAYING UNDERNEATH ME.

NO WAY AM I GOING TO GO BACK INTO BLOODCLAN TERRITORY, ESPECIALLY NOT TONIGHT. ALL I WANT TO DO IS REST.

ARE YOU THE MAN WITH THE SHIP'S CAT?

UHH... BEG YOUR PARDON?

MY SON'S FRIEND HERE SAID SOMETHING ABOUT YOUR BOAT HAVING A CAT ON IT.

HE WOULDN'T REST UNTIL WE ALL CAME DOWN HERE TO SEE THE THING.

DARREL'S JUST MAD ABOUT PIRATES, YOU SEE. HE'D LOVE TO MEET A REAL SHIP'S CAT.

BUT NOW THAT EVERYBODY'S GOING...I GUESS THAT MEANS I HAVE TO GO, TOO?

YEAH...THE CAPTAIN'S HEADING TO HIS DEN.

I'LL TRY NOT TO MAKE ANY NOISE WHEN I LEAVE THIS TIME.

WHICH WAY NOW? I MIGHT BE ABLE TO FIND MORE NICE HOUSEFOLK BACK TOWARD TWOLEGPLACE. MAYBE.

OR MAYBE I COULD FOLLOW THE WATER, TO WHERE I SAW THE TREES AND THOSE GIANT THINGS WITH HORNS.

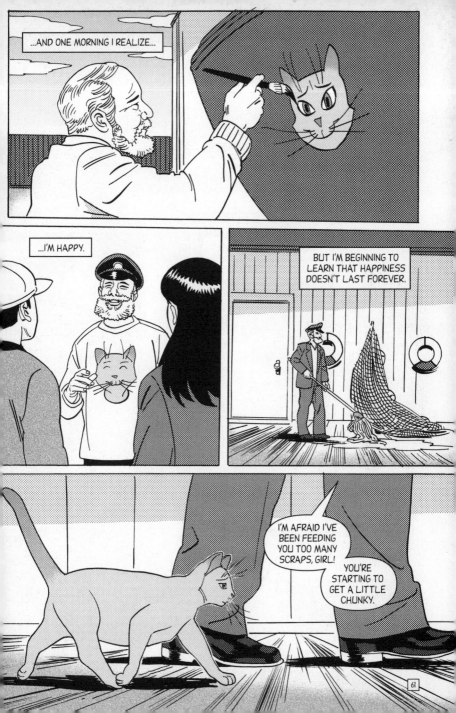

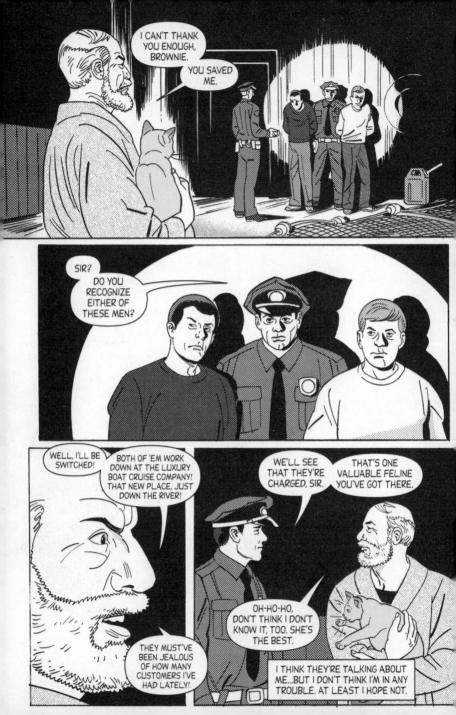

I'VE ONLY HEARD ABOUT THIS. I'VE NEVER SEEN IT. IT'S A LITTLE HARD TO BELIEVE, UNTIL I DO SEE IT.

BUT THERE IT IS. THE WHOLE RIVER HAS FROZEN OVER.

WAAA-HAAAA!

IT'S NOT SOLID, THOUGH. THERE'S STILL FRIGID WATER UNDERNEATH. I CAN SMELL IT...

AND I CAN HEAR THE CREAKING AS WEIGHT SHIFTS ON IT.

PATCH!

PATCH, IT'S NOT SAFE OUT THERE! COME BACK TO THE SHORE!

O-OKAY, SASHA...I'M COMING...

ERIN HUNTER

is inspired by a love of cats and a fascination with the ferocity of the natural world. As well as having great respect for nature in all its forms, Erin enjoys creating rich mythical explanations for animal behavior. She is also the author of the Seekers series.

Visit the Clans online
and play Warriors games at
www.warriorcats.com.

For exclusive information on your
favorite authors and artists, visit
www.authortracker.com.

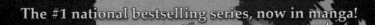

WARRIORS

TIGERSTAR & SASHA

RETURN TO THE CLANS

ERIN HUNTER

KEEP WATCH FOR

WARRIORS

TIGERSTAR & SASHA
#3: RETURN TO THE CLANS

Sasha has gone back to the forest to raise her kits, Moth, Hawk, and Tadpole. She thinks she's a safe distance from ShadowClan's prying eyes, but Tigerstar still haunts her dreams, and Sasha fears that he will soon discover the existence of his kits. As leaf-bare stretches on, and Sasha finds it harder to feed her family, she wonders if her kits might be better off as warriors, with a Clan to protect and train them. But where does Sasha belong?

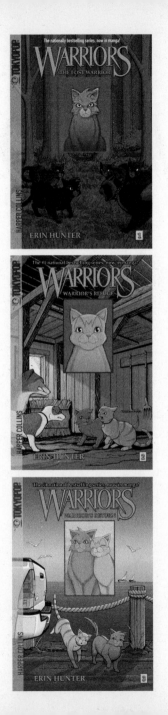

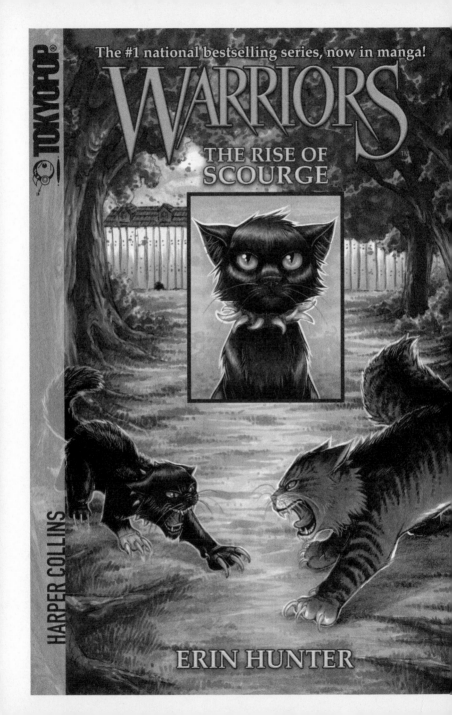

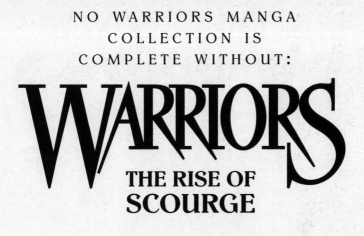

WARRIORS

THE RISE OF
SCOURGE

Black-and-white Tiny may be the runt of the litter, but he's also the most curious about what lies beyond the backyard fence. When he crosses paths with some wild cats defending their territory, Tiny is left with scars—and a bitter, deep-seated grudge—that he carries with him back to Twolegplace. As his reputation grows among the strays and loners that live in the dirty brick alleyways, Tiny leaves behind his name, his kittypet past, and everything that was once important to him—except his deadly desire for revenge.

WARRIORS

CATS of the CLANS

ERIN HUNTER

ILLUSTRATED BY WAYNE McLOUGHLIN

MEET THE CLANS' HEROES IN

WARRIORS
CATS of the CLANS

Hear the stories of the great warriors as they've never
been told before! Chock-full of visual treats and cap-
tivating details, including full-color illustrations and
in-depth biographies of important cats from all four
Clans, from fierce Clan leaders to wise medicine cats
to the most mischievous kits.

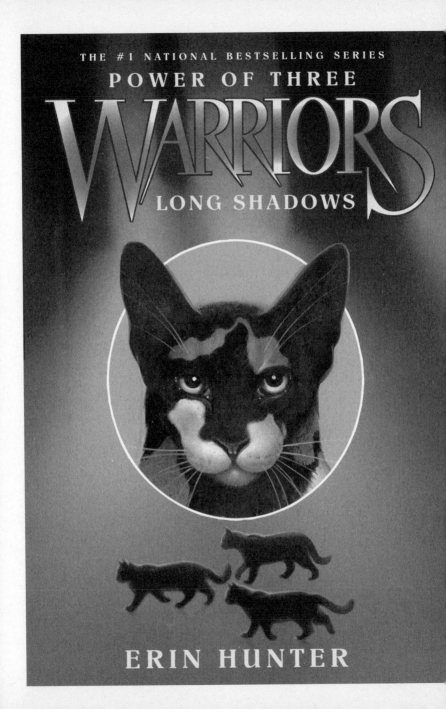

POWER OF THREE

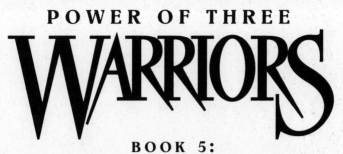

WARRIORS

BOOK 5:

LONG SHADOWS

TURN THE PAGE FOR A PEEK
AT THE NEXT WARRIORS NOVEL,
*WARRIORS: POWER OF THREE
#5: LONG SHADOWS.*

Blackstar has declared that ShadowClan will no longer
follow StarClan, which throws the rest of the Clans into
turmoil. Should they, too, abandon the warrior code?
Jaypaw believes that their ancestors still have a place
in the cats' lives, but there are questions that can't be
answered by StarClan alone. Determined to discover
the truth about the cats' history, Jaypaw finds he must
look deep into events long-buried in time, farther back
than even StarClan can remember. . . .

CHAPTER 1

The moon was huge, a golden circle resting on a dark ridge of hills. Stars blazed above Hollyleaf's head, reminding her that the spirits of her ancestors were watching over her. Her fur prickled as something stirred on the ridge. A cat had appeared there, outlined against the moon. She recognized the broad head and tufted ears, and the tail with its bushy tip; even though the shape was black against the light, she knew the colors of its pelt: white with brown, black, and ginger blotches.

"*Sol!*" she hissed.

The outlined shape arched its back, then reared up on its hind paws, its forepaws stretched out as if it was about to rake its claws across the sky. It leaped upward, and as it leaped it swelled until it was so huge that it blotted out the moon and the blazing stars. Hollyleaf crouched, shivering, in darkness thicker than the deepest places of the forest.

Screeches of alarm rose up around her, a whole Clan of hidden cats wailing their fear of the shadow cutting them off from the protective gaze of StarClan. Above the noise, a single voice rang out: "Hollyleaf! Hollyleaf! Come out!"

Hollyleaf thrashed in terror and found her paws tangled in soft moss and bracken. Pale gray light was filtering through the branches of the warriors' den. A couple of foxlengths away, Hazeltail was scrambling out of her nest, shaking scraps of moss from her pelt.

"Hollyleaf!" The call came again, and this time Hollyleaf recognized Birchfall's voice, meowing irritably outside the den. "Are you going to sleep all day? We're supposed to be hunting."

"Coming." Groggy with sleep, every hair on her pelt still quivering from her nightmare, Hollyleaf headed toward the nearest gap between the branches. Before she reached it, her paws stumbled over the haunches of a sleeping cat, half hidden under the bracken.

Cloudtail's head popped up. "Great StarClan!" he grumbled. "Can't a cat get any sleep around here?"

"S-sorry," Hollyleaf stammered, remembering that Cloudtail had been out on a late patrol the night before; she had seen him return to camp with Dustpelt and Sorreltail while she was keeping her warrior's vigil.

Just my luck. My first day, and I manage to annoy one of the senior warriors!

Cloudtail snorted and curled up again, his blue eyes closing as he buried his nose in his fur.

"It's okay," Hazeltail murmured, brushing her muzzle

against Hollyleaf's shoulder. "Cloudtail's mew is worse than his scratch. And don't let Birchfall ruffle your fur. He's bossy with the new warriors, but you'll soon get used to it."

Hollyleaf nodded gratefully, though she didn't tell Hazeltail the real reason she was thrown off balance. Birchfall didn't bother her; it was the memory of the dream that throbbed through her from ears to tail-tip, making her paws clumsy and her thoughts troubled.

Her gaze drifted to the nest where her brother Lion-paw—no, Lion*blaze* now—had curled up at the end of his vigil. She wanted to talk to him more than anything. But the nest was empty; Lionblaze must have gone out on the dawn patrol.

Careful where she put her paws, Hollyleaf pushed her way out of the den behind Hazeltail. Outside, Birch-fall was scraping the ground impatiently.

"At last!" he snapped. "What kept you?"

"Take it easy, Birchfall." Brambleclaw, the ThunderClan deputy and Hollyleaf's father, was sitting a tail-length away with his tail wrapped neatly around his paws. His amber eyes were calm. "The prey won't run away."

"Not till they see us, anyway," Sandstorm added as she bounded across from the fresh-kill pile.

"If there is any prey." Birchfall lashed his tail. "Ever since the battle, fresh-kill's been much harder to find."

Hollyleaf's grumbling belly told her that Birchfall

was right. Several sunrises ago all four Clans had battled in ThunderClan territory; their screeching and trampling had frightened off all the prey, or driven them deep underground.

"Maybe the prey will start to come back now," she suggested.

"Maybe," Brambleclaw agreed. "We'll head toward the ShadowClan border. There wasn't as much fighting over there."

Hollyleaf stiffened at the mention of ShadowClan. *Will I see Sol again?* she wondered.

"I wonder if we'll see any ShadowClan cats," Birchfall meowed, echoing her thought. "I'd like to know if they're all going to turn their back on StarClan, and follow that weirdo loner instead."

Hollyleaf felt as if stones were dragging in her belly, weighing her down. ShadowClan had not appeared at the last Gathering, two nights before. Instead, their leader Blackstar had come alone except for Sol, the loner who had recently arrived by the lake, and explained that his cats no longer believed in the power of their warrior ancestors.

But that can't be right! How can a Clan survive without Star-Clan? Without the warrior code?

"Sol's not such a weirdo," Hazeltail pointed out to Birchfall with a flick of her ears. "He predicted that the sun would vanish, and it did. None of the medicine cats knew that was going to happen."

Birchfall shrugged. "The sun came back, didn't it? It's not that big a deal."

"In any case," Brambleclaw interrupted, rising to his paws, "this is a hunting patrol. We're not going to pay a friendly visit to ShadowClan."

"But they fought beside us," Birchfall objected. "WindClan and RiverClan would have turned us into crow-food without the ShadowClan warriors. We can't be enemies again so soon, can we?"

"Not enemies," Sandstorm corrected. "But they're still a different Clan. Besides, I'm not sure we can be friends with cats who reject StarClan."

What about our own cats, then? Hollyleaf didn't dare to ask the question out loud. *Cloudtail has never believed in Star-Clan.* But she knew without question Cloudtail was a loyal warrior who would die for any of his Clanmates.

Brambleclaw said nothing, just gave his pelt a shake and kinked his tail to beckon the rest of the patrol. As they headed toward the thorn tunnel they met Bracken-fur pushing his way into the hollow with Sorreltail and Lionblaze behind him. The dawn patrol had returned. As all three cats headed for the fresh-kill pile, Hollyleaf darted across and intercepted her brother.

"How did it go? Is there anything to report?"

Lionblaze's jaws parted in a huge yawn. *He must be exhausted,* Hollyleaf thought, *after keeping his warrior vigil and then being chosen for the dawn patrol.*

"Not a thing," he mewed, shaking his head. "All's

quiet on the WindClan border."

"We're going over toward ShadowClan territory." Alone with her brother, Hollyleaf could confess how worried she was. "I'm scared we'll meet Sol. What if he tells the other cats about the prophecy?"

Lionblaze pressed his muzzle into her shoulder. "Come on! Is it likely that Sol will be doing border patrols? He'll be lying around the ShadowClan camp, stuffing himself with fresh-kill."

Hollyleaf shook her head. "I don't know . . . I just wish we'd never told him anything."

"So do I." Lionblaze's eyes narrowed and his tone was bitter as he went on. "But it's not like Sol is bothered about us. He decided to stay with Blackstar, didn't he? He promised to help us after we told him about the prophecy, but he soon changed his mind."

"We're better off without him." Hollyleaf swiped her tongue over her brother's ear.

"Hollyleaf!"

She spun around to see Brambleclaw waiting beside the entrance to the thorn tunnel, the tip of his tail twitching impatiently.

"I've got to go," she meowed to Lionblaze, and raced across the clearing to join Brambleclaw. "Sorry," she gasped, and plunged into the tunnel.

The morning had been raw and cold, but as Holly-leaf padded through the forest with her Clanmates the clouds began to clear away. Long claws of sunlight pierced the branches, tipping the leaves with fire where they had changed from green to red and gold. Leaf-fall was almost upon them.

ENTER THE WORLD OF
WARRIORS

Warriors

Sinister perils threaten the four warrior Clans. Into the midst of this turmoil comes Rusty, an ordinary housecat, who may just be the bravest of them all.

Warriors: The New Prophecy

Follow the next generation of heroic cats as they set off on a quest to save the Clans from destruction.

ENTER THE WORLD OF
WARRIORS

Warriors: Power of Three
Firestar's grandchildren begin their training as warrior cats.
Prophecy foretells that they will hold more power than any cats before them.

Delve Deeper into the Clans

Warrior Cats Come to Life in Manga!

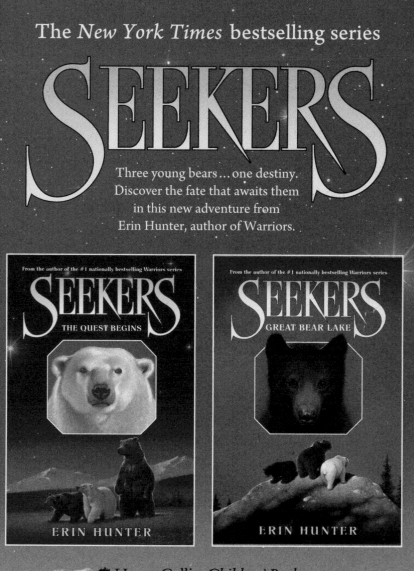